BY MICHAEL DAHL

ILLUSTRATED BY BRADFORD KENDALL

Librarian Reviewer
Laurie K. Holland
Media Specialist

Reading Consultant
Elizabeth Stedem
Educator/Consultant

Raintree is an imprint of Capstone Global Library Limited, a company incorporated in England and Wales having its registered office at 7 Pilgrim Street, London, EC4V 6LB – Registered company number: 6695582

"Raintree" is a registered trademark of Pearson Education Limited, under licence to Capstone Global Library Limited

First published by Stone Arch Books in 2008
First published in hardback in the United Kingdom in 2009
First published in paperback in the United Kingdom in 2010

Creative Director: Heather Kinseth
Senior Designer for Cover and Interior: Kay Fraser
Graphic Designer: Brann Garvey
Edited in the UK by Laura Knowles
Printed and bound in China by Leo Paper Products Ltd

ISBN 978-1406212785 (hardback)
13 12 11 10 09
10 9 8 7 6 5 4 3 2 1

ISBN 978-1406212648 (paperback)
14 13 12 11 10
10 9 8 7 6 5 4 3 2 1

British Library Cataloguing in Publication Data
Dahl, Michael.
The word eater. -- (Library of doom)
813.5'4-dc22
A full catalogue record for this book is available from the British Library.

TABLE OF CONTENTS

The Library of Doom is the world's largest collection of strange and dangerous books. The Librarian's duty is to keep the books from falling into the hands of those who would use them for evil purposes.

CHAPTER 1

A SILVER STAB

On a **windy** afternoon, a young man **walks** through a market.

The young man has money in his pocket.

He walks by tables **piled** with old books for sale.

He finds a **strange book** at the **bottom** of one pile.

It has **sharp corners** that are made of silver.

The title of the book is *Full Moon Monster.*

The man **looks up** at the sky. It is getting **darker.**

"There will be a **full moon** tonight," he thinks.

"Ouch!"

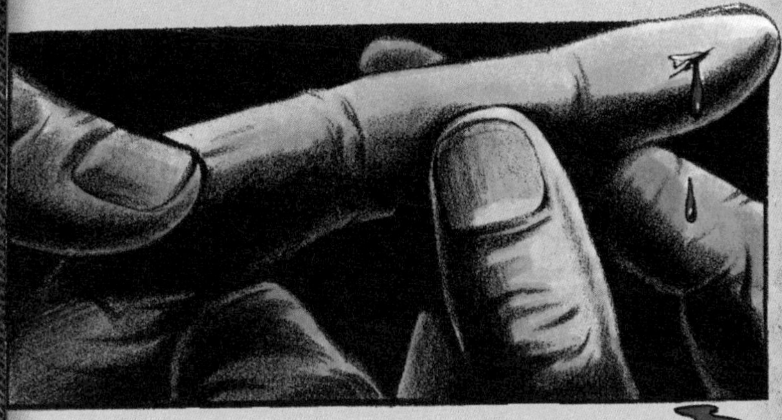

One of the book's silver corners has **poked** the man's finger.

He begins to **bleed.**

A small piece of silver is **stuck** in his skin.

CHAPTER 2

A NEW CREATURE

The young man buys the book and then **walks home.**

Soon, he feels **hot** and **sweaty.**

"I must have a **fever**," he thinks.

He **stops** to rest against a tree in the park.

The moon **shines** brightly through the waving tree branches.

The young man **falls** to the ground.

His hair grows into long, **stiff fur.**

His fingers become **claws.** His backbone arches.

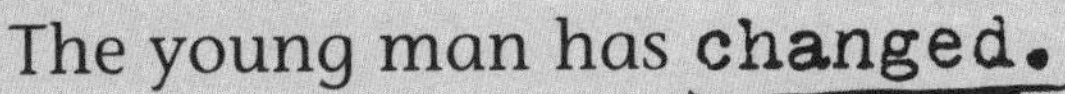

The young man has **changed.**

Now, a strange **new** creature moves among the trees.

CHAPTER 3

The next morning, the young man **wakes up** in his apartment.

Piles of old books lie around him.

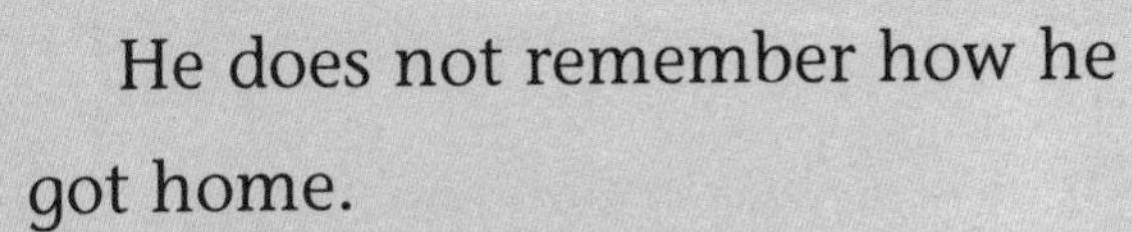

He does not remember how he got home.

He does not know how the books got there, either.

When he opens the books, he sees something **terrifying.**

All the words are **missing.**

CHAPTER 4

That night, a strange creature **prowls** through the city streets.

The beast **smashes** through the market.

It rips apart the **locked bins** of books.

The creature grabs a book in its **terrible claws.** Its long, twisting tongue licks the pages.

When it has eaten all the words, the creature **tosses** the book aside.

Then it grabs another book.

The creature stomps by a house with a mailbox in front of it.

It **licks** the name off the mailbox.

Suddenly, everyone in the house disappears.

"That's enough!" a strong voice yells.

CHAPTER 5

THE FACE OFF

A tall, **dark shadow** appears in front of the creature.

It is the **Librarian.**

"This has gone on long enough," says the man.

"I order you to **return** to your original shape."

The creature **snarls** at the Librarian.

It is still hungry.

The creature bends down and begins to **scratch** in the **soil**.

The creature **spells** words in the soil.

Then the creature's long tongue whips out and **licks** at the letters.

The Librarian looks down at his body.

He begins to **fade away.**

The creature **roars** with **laughter.**

Its laughter sounds like books being **ripped** apart.

The Librarian has almost completely **vanished.**

Only one of his hands is left.

The Librarian's hand **reaches** towards the creature.

The hand grabs one of the creature's fingers.

It is the finger that has a small piece of silver stuck in it.

Then, the Librarian **disappears.**

He is gone.

But the creature's finger, with the silver splinter, is also **gone.**

Suddenly, the creature falls to the ground.

Its back grows shorter. Its claws turn into **human hands.**

The man **wonders** how he got there.

Then he hears **voices** and laughter in the dark.

In a house not too far away, people are **appearing** again.

Far away, in the Library of Doom, the **Librarian** appears.

In his hand he holds a **silver splinter.**

A PAGE FROM THE LIBRARY OF DOOM

Legends and folklore from around the world tell tales of humans who change their shapes. One of the best known shape shifters is the **werewolf** (WAIR-wulf). This is a human who turns into a wolf at night, and then back into a human at daybreak.

The ability to turn into a wolf is called **lycanthropy** (ly-KAN-throp-ee).

You become a werewolf if you are bitten by one. But some people believed that if they wore the skin of a wolf at night, they might be transformed into the beast.

If a werewolf is struck by iron or silver, it will die. The creature will turn back into a human.

According to legend, the best month for turning into a werewolf is February. The best day is Saturday.

How can you tell if a person is really a werewolf? Look at their left thumb. If the thumbnail is extra long, watch out!

You can cure a werewolf by throwing another wolf skin onto it, but with the hair on the inside.

In countries where there are no wolves, people tell legends about other shape shifters. In China there are were-tigers, in Japan there are were-foxes, in Africa there are were-crocodiles and were-lions.

ABOUT THE AUTHOR

Michael Dahl is the author of more than 100 books for children and young adults. He has twice won the AEP Distinguished Achievement Award for his non-fiction. His Finnegan Zwake mystery series was chosen by the Agatha Awards to be among the five best mystery books for children in 2002 and 2003. He collects books on poison and graveyards, and lives in a haunted house in Minneapolis, USA.

ABOUT THE ILLUSTRATOR

Bradford Kendall has enjoyed drawing for as long as he can remember. As a boy, he loved to read comic books and watch old monster films. He graduated from the Rhode Island School of Design with a BFA in Illustration. He has owned his own commercial art business since 1983, and lives in Providence, Rhode Island, USA, with his wife, Leigh, and their two children Lily and Stephen. They also have a cat named Hansel and a dog named Gretel.

GLOSSARY

beast (BEEST) – a wild animal or monster

fever (FEE-vur) – a higher than normal body temperature. People often get a fever when they are sick.

market (MAR-kit) – a place where people meet to buy or sell goods

prowls (PROULZ) – to move quietly, like an animal hunting for food

snarl (SNARL) – to show teeth angrily

splinter (SPLIN-tur) – a small, thin piece of wood, metal, or other material that can stick into the skin

terrifying (TER-uh-fye-ing) – extremely frightening or scary

vanish (VAN-ish) – to disappear without warning

DISCUSSION QUESTIONS

1. What's the strangest book you've ever read? Describe the cover of the book and what the book was about.

2. At the end of the story, the young man hears voices. It is the sound of people appearing back in their house. What had happened to them? Why did they reappear?

3. Imagine you could only save one word from the jaws of the Word Eater. What word would it be and why?

WRITING PROMPTS

1. The Librarian stopped the Word Eater, but the *Full Moon Monster* book is still around. Write a story about what will happen to the next person who finds it.

2. Choosing the right words can be the most difficult part of writing. So, have someone do it for you! Ask a friend to make a list of 10 words. Your mission is to write a story using all the words on that list.

3. Describe the strangest item you've ever bought, received, or found. Why was this object so strange? What did it look like? Do you still have it?

MORE BOOKS TO READ

This story may be over, but there are many more dangerous adventures in store for the Librarian. Will the Librarian be able to escape the cave of the deadly giant bookworms? Will he stop the smashing scroll in time to save the world? You can only find out by reading the other books from the Library of Doom...

Attack of the Paper Bats

The Beast Beneath the Stairs

The Book that Dripped Blood

Cave of the Bookworms

The Creeping Bookends

Escape from the Pop-up Prison

The Eye in the Graveyard

The Golden Book of Death

Poison Pages

The Smashing Scroll

The Twister Trap